This book
belongs to

..........................

For Anya, my smashing little girl

FREDERICK WARNE

Published by the Penguin Group
Penguin Books Ltd, 80 Strand, London WC2R oRL, England
Penguin Young Readers Group, 345 Hudson Street,
New York, New York 10014, U.S.A.
Penguin Books Australia Ltd, 250 Camberwell Road, Camberwell,
Victoria 3124, Australia
Canada, India, New Zealand, South Africa

1 3 5 7 9 10 8 6 4 2

ISBN-13: 978 07232 6285 5

Printed in Great Britain

# Tansy's New Petals

by Kay Woodward

# Welcome to the Flower Fairies' Garden!

Where are the fairies?
Where can we find them?
We've seen the fairy-rings
They leave behind them!

Is it a secret
No one is telling?
Why, in your garden
Surely they're dwelling!

No need for journeying,
Seeking afar:
Where there are flowers,
There fairies are!

# Contents

Once upon a time, there was a cluster of pretty flowers that grew right in the middle of the Flower Fairies' Garden. Each flower was the color of sunshine and no bigger than a fairy's hand. And the Flower Fairy who cared for them was called Tansy—a pretty creature who wore a simple yellow dress made from her own petals. A garland of fine, green leaves encircled her golden-brown hair.

A long time ago, tansy flowers were very popular,

especially with humans. Great chefs and cooks used them to make tasty tansy puddings and crumbly tansy cake. Nurses made tansy posset, which was a hot, sloppy drink guaranteed to revive even the feeblest patient. But Candytuft Fairy—who was famous throughout Flower Fairyland for her sweets—made perhaps the most enchanting treat of all. She whisked the bright yellow flowers together with fresh dew to make tansy toffee. It was so gooey that everyone's teeth stuck together.

"Deeeelicious!" All the Flower Fairies said, once they could speak again.

With her flowers in such demand, Tansy was always kept busy making sure that her plants were wonderfully neat and tidy. She trimmed back the ragged leaves, which could easily go wild if they were left, and whisked away any spotted old petals that she came across. Every morning she sprinkled fairy dust on the flowers to make them glow and, during dry spells, she watered the soil at dawn and dusk. She simply adored the fact that everyone loved her flowers and did her best to make sure they were always in tip-top condition.

Time passed.

Recipes changed.

Chefs and cooks no longer dropped by to pick tansy flowers for their puddings, cakes, and their possets.

"What's going on . . . ?" Tansy complained to a visiting blackbird, who shrugged his feathers and flew away.

Confused and upset, Tansy knew that she needed to investigate. So she crept towards the house at the top of the garden, making quite sure that no one spotted her. (The Flower Fairy Law said that fairies must stay out of sight at all times. If humans knew that fairies really did exist, the Flower Fairies' secret world would be in danger.) With a flutter of creamy yellow wings, Tansy flew up to the basket of anemones and daisies that hung from the wall of

the house. And then the strangest words drifted through the open kitchen window ...

"*Banoffi pie ...*"

Tansy wrinkled her forehead.
She didn't have a clue what a banoffi
was, but it sounded like just the sort of
weird and wonderful thing that humans
would like to eat.

"*Millionaire's shortbread ...*"

Goodness! If humans were cooking
with real gold now, it was no wonder

they had abandoned
Tansy's flowers.
Sadly, she fluttered
down to the ground
and trudged back to
her home. It gave
her some
small

comfort to know that Candytuft still used the little golden flowers to make toffee, but she alone couldn't use as many petals as Tansy grew.

Quickly, the jagged green leaves and button-like flowers grew out of control, racing across the ground towards Lavender, Zinnia, and Rose, and threatening to swamp the other flowers too. No matter how much Tansy clipped and snipped and

trimmed and
pruned, she
couldn't keep up
with her precious plant.
It was out of control.
"I'm terribly sorry,
Tansy, but you'll have to
do something about it," said
Lavender anxiously. "Soon, yours will
be the only flower in the Flower Fairies'
Garden. There'll be no room for
anything else."

"I know . . . " said Tansy,
her usually sunny face
creased with worry.
"I'm trying my best,
I am really."

But her
best wasn't
good enough.

And one awful day, her worst fears came true. A brightly dressed visitor waded through the sea of bright tansy flowers that now stretched from Lavender's delicate stems right across to the sweet peas. It was Dandelion, his beautiful yellow and black wings dazzling her with their brilliance.

The stunning Flower Fairy rubbed his chin thoughtfully before he spoke.

"I'm afraid that I'm the bearer of bad tidings," he said seriously.

Tansy nodded. She could guess what was coming and she knew that she wasn't going to like it one bit.

"It's not that we don't love you dearly," said Dandelion. "We all do—me, Lavender, Poppy ... It's just that there simply isn't enough room for your flowers. There are far too many of them."

"N-n-nobody picks them anymore," wailed Tansy. "And I just can't keep them under control." A single tear rolled down her cheek.

Dandelion bent down and gave her a neatly folded yellow petal from his flower to use as a handkerchief. "There, there," he said, as Tansy blew her nose.

"You want me to leave Flower Fairyland, don't you?" she sobbed. "I'm to be banished into the mysterious beyond!"

"No, not at all!" Dandelion shook his head briskly from side to side. "Of course we don't want you to leave Flower Fairyland... but the other fairies and I were wondering if you might like to relocate to the King's Highway, just over the garden wall.

There's plenty of room for your lovely flowers to spread out there. And I know White Bindweed will make you very welcome. And we'll only ever be on the other side of the wall!"

Tansy sniffed and gave a brave nod. There wasn't really much more to say. It was time to go.

## Chapter Two
# On the King's Highway

Tansy plumped up her cushion, which
was made from large bindweed petals sewn
together and stuffed with feathers, and sank
into its softness. Dreamily, she closed her
eyes and imagined she was floating on a
fluffy cloud.

"Aaaaah," she sighed contentedly.

She needn't have worried. The King's Highway—a country lane that was the main route between the Flower Fairies' Garden and the marshes—was wilder than she was used to, but it was a wonderful place to live.

The Flower Fairies who lived beside the King's Highway were just as friendly as those in the garden. White Bindweed had been wonderful —introducing Tansy to all the other fairies of the wayside and showing her the sights. And there was always something to see. Fairies fluttered up and down the lane as they

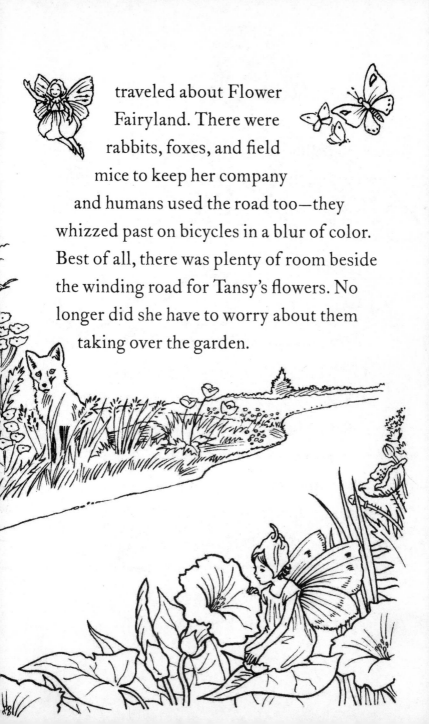

traveled about Flower Fairyland. There were rabbits, foxes, and field mice to keep her company and humans used the road too—they whizzed past on bicycles in a blur of color. Best of all, there was plenty of room beside the winding road for Tansy's flowers. No longer did she have to worry about them taking over the garden.

"Oy!" The silence was shattered by a gruff voice.

Tansy sat bolt upright in surprise, her emerald eyes pinging open to see who had spoken.

It was an elf! From the peak of his pointy hat to the tips of his tiny slippers, the strange little creature was dressed entirely in green. He scowled, and leaned forward to look at her more closely.

"Who are you?" he said rudely. "You're new round these parts, aren't you?"

"Er, yes," admitted Tansy. "But Dandelion gave me permission to live here—"

"Dandelion? Pah!" scoffed the elf. "Who does he think he is, anyway? A fairy estate agent? Strutting about in his bumblebee outfit, bossing everyone around, deciding who can do what and who can live where. I suppose he thinks that he owns the road, too." The angry elf stomped back and forth on the edge of the King's Highway, kicking at the ground and coughing as dust billowed up around him.

Softly, Tansy explained about her flowers.
"... And so there wasn't room for me any
more," she finished. "Dandelion thought
I might be more at home here.
He's a very caring fairy,
you see."

"Hmph," huffed the elf.

Tansy noticed that his ragged
jacket had two buttons missing.
A single button, made from
a dried blackberry,
hung from a thread.
"Would you like me
to fix that for you?"
she asked. Unlike many
of the Flower Fairies,
she loved sewing. And
besides, she was keen
to find a way to stop
the elf complaining

about Dandelion. (Flower Fairies are very loyal. They can't stand to hear a bad word said about another fairy.)

The elf stopped his angry dance at once. "Really?" he said, his pursed lips widening into a huge grin. "Ooh, yes please!" In an instant, he whipped off his tattered jacket and stuffed it into Tansy's hands. Promising to return the following day, he scampered

away before she could change her mind.

Smiling to herself, Tansy reached for the
small nutshell that she always kept close at
hand. It contained her sewing kit—a pair of
shiny scissors, a reel of flaxen thread, and
a tiny pink cushion bristling with pins.
The Flower Fairy clucked as she examined
the elf's jacket. It was in a dreadful state . . .
But with a nip and a tuck here, and a sprinkle
of fairy dust there, it would look as good
as new. As she touched the last blackberry,

it crumbled away and Tansy wondered
where she'd get more berries at this time
of year. Unless . . .

"Of course!" she exclaimed aloud.
All around her were clusters of small,
round, yellow flowers. Her tansy
flowers would make excellent buttons.
At last—she'd found another use for
them! Without further ado, she picked up her
sewing needle and a length of the finest flax
and set to work. And as she worked, she sang:

*"Still I'm here by the King's Highway,*
*Where the air from the fields*
*Is fresh and sweet,*
*With my fine-cut leaves and my flowers neat.*
*Were ever such button-like flowers seen—*
*Yellow, for elfin coats of green?"*

The elf was delighted with his new buttons and soon told all his friends about Tansy. It wasn't long before she was swamped with polite requests from the other elves.

"May I please have some new buttons too?"

"Any chance you could add a row of tansy flowers around the hem of my

tunic . . . and on my shoes . . . and on my hat?"

"I'd simply adore some tansy-flower cufflinks . . ."

Tansy and the elves were soon the best of friends. To thank her for the sewing repairs and the fashion advice that she often gave them, they brought her small gifts—usually things that humans had left behind them. Ribbons, sequins, dainty handkerchiefs . . . Before long, Tansy had a huge collection of pretty bits and bobs. She tucked the beautiful things safely away until she could think of something special to do with them.

As she ran her fingers over the leafy fabric of another elf's jacket—her seventeenth that week—Tansy realized that she'd completely changed her mind about the strange little creatures. Certainly, she'd heard lots of stories about the naughty tricks elves had played on the Flower Fairies, but she couldn't believe her new friends would make such mischief. They were polite and went out of their way to make sure that Tansy was happy in her new home. Only last week, a particularly gruff elf had insisted that he fan her with a dock leaf to keep her cool in the hot weather.

As far as she was concerned, the elves were wonderful. So why did everyone else think that they were such a nuisance?

# Chapter Three
## A Mischievous Plan

A short distance from Tansy's new home, there grew a circle of beautiful toadstools. The chocolate-brown stems and red-and-white caps looked good enough to eat, but the Flower Fairies knew not to go anywhere near these particular toadstools. It was said they were quite poisonous. This made them the perfect spot for the elves' hideaway.

Today, a top-secret meeting was in progress...

"It's the truth, I tell you," whispered a large elf. "She's been evicted from the Flower Fairies' Garden."

"No!" cried the small elf with red hair and freckles who was crouched next to him. "Lovely Tansy? You're making it up!'

The chief elf shook his head solemnly. "I wish I were," he said. "But it's true. She's been exiled ... expelled ... *banished.*"

"*Why?*" shouted a medium-sized elf, who wore a small moustache. "Who would do such a thing?"

So the chief elf explained. Poor Tansy's petals were no longer

as popular as they had once been, it seemed.
Those pesky humans, who were always
changing their minds about what they
liked and what they didn't like, had
decided that they preferred banoffi pie
to tansy pudding. "What's a banoffi?"
asked the small, ginger elf.

"Dunno." The medium-sized elf shrugged.
The chief elf patted his round tummy and
smiled. "It's a pie made from banana and
toffee, of course," he announced grandly.
"I once saw the humans from the big house
making one. When they left the
kitchen for a moment I crept in
and had a taste." He licked
his lips thoughtfully then
went on to explain that
the Flower Fairies had

decided Tansy's flowers were too wild for them. "So they booted her out," he finished.

"What can we do?" questioned the medium-sized elf, who liked everyone to be treated fairly.

The chief elf tapped his nose. "I have a plan," he said.

It was a plan so simple, yet so utterly brilliant that the other elves were speechless with delight. So their beloved Tansy had been thrown out of the Flower Fairies' Garden because there wasn't enough room for her, had she? Well, they would *make* room for her.

That night, after the sun had set, the three elves crept into the Flower Fairies' Garden. First slinging a rope over the wall, they clambered up and over, hoisting their tools after them. The chief elf carried a spade.

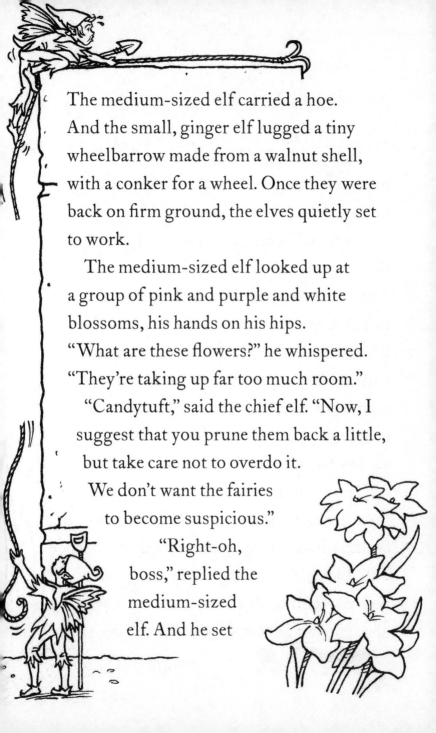

The medium-sized elf carried a hoe.
And the small, ginger elf lugged a tiny
wheelbarrow made from a walnut shell,
with a conker for a wheel. Once they were
back on firm ground, the elves quietly set
to work.

The medium-sized elf looked up at
a group of pink and purple and white
blossoms, his hands on his hips.
"What are these flowers?" he whispered.
"They're taking up far too much room."

"Candytuft," said the chief elf. "Now, I
suggest that you prune them back a little,
but take care not to overdo it.
We don't want the fairies
to become suspicious."

"Right-oh,
boss," replied the
medium-sized
elf. And he set

about snipping at the outermost flowers.

The smallest elf rolled past, his wheelbarrow piled high with dandelion clocks. The wispy seeds floated away on the night breeze. "Hey," he said. "Guess what time it is!"

"Half-past eight?"

"Time to get rid of these tired old flowers!" said the little elf. He headed in the direction of the compost heap, laughing quietly at his own joke.

The elves worked until the moon hung high in the night sky. Then they hid their tools under the mulberry bush and headed back over the wall to their home on the marsh. The garden they left behind looked only slightly different from the one they had entered earlier that evening. But it *was* different. There was a little more space here and a little less foliage there. The question was—would anyone notice?

At first, the Flower Fairies didn't realize that anything was going on. Life carried on pretty much the same as usual. Poppy did say to Sweet Pea that the garden was looking very tidy, while Candytuft noticed that her flowers seemed neater than usual. Dandelion told everyone that it must have been very windy, because his dandelion clocks had blown away. But that was all.

Night after night, the elves continued their visits. Next, they decided to make some room in the old, wooden greenhouse in a sunny spot at the bottom of the Flower Fairies' Garden. Inside, there were a few plant pots dotted about the shelves. Some held frilly white and rose fuschias. In other pots, tiny seedlings grew.

"Look at all that wasted shelf space!" announced the medium-sized elf. "Why, if we rearranged them a little, there would be heaps of room for more flowers to grow. There must be more Flower Fairies who'd prefer the warmth of the greenhouse to living outdoors. Perhaps some of them might even like to come here on holiday!"

"Splendid idea," said the chief elf. "Let's get cracking."

So, huffing and puffing as they heaved

plant pots to and fro, the three elves tidied up the greenhouse. And, sure enough, there was plenty of space for more Flower Fairies and their flowers to live.

Little by little, the elves filled up the shelves. Just a sunflower here and a peony there ... Not so many flowers that the fairies would notice, but enough to make room for Tansy. In fact, it went so well, that the elves grew even bolder. Now, they didn't just move the odd flower— they relocated whole bunches of them.

"This marigold is rather in the way,"
said the medium-sized elf. "Don't you think
it would look better near the lavender bush?"

"Good thinking," said the chief elf.
"Then we could shift the periwinkles too."

"I say," said the smallest elf. "Does anyone
really like dog-violets? I know I don't . . .
Why don't we hide them behind the
rose bush?"

Slowly but surely, the Flower Fairies' home

began to change. The flowers were moved outwards until a small clearing appeared in the center of the garden. The small clearing grew into a medium-sized clearing, which became a big clearing in no time at all.

Soon, it was big enough to host the annual Midsummer Party.

And at long last, the Flower Fairies noticed.

"What is *that*?" cried a horrified Lavender.

Dandelion, who just happened to be strolling past at that moment, stopped dead in his tracks. "What is *what*?" he asked. Then he stared at the dusty patch of ground, where Lavender was pointing. "Why, there's nothing there," he said. "What's the problem?"

"The problem, my dear Dandelion," said Lavender patiently, "is that this empty space used to be filled with flowers. And I'd like to know where they've gone!"

Meanwhile, Tansy had decided that life on the King's Highway wasn't quite as exciting as she'd hoped. The Flower Fairies who'd been dropping by to

visit her new home had
suddenly stopped coming.
Tansy was astonished.
How could they forget
her so quickly?

As for her new friends,
the elves, well, they weren't
half so much fun as they used to be.
They always seemed to be tired and
grumpy nowadays. And the bags under
their eyes were big enough to pack all their
belongings in. But whenever Tansy asked
them why they were so sleepy, they looked
sheepish and changed the subject.

So, with no one to play with and only
White Bindweed for company, Tansy
had more spare time than she'd ever
thought possible. So, she decided to
do the one thing that she'd always wanted
to do. She was going to follow her dreams.

One by one, the Flower Fairies discovered that someone had been landscaping their precious garden without their permission. And then there was chaos.

"How dare they?" stormed Herb Robert, a fairy with ears so pointy he might have been an elf.

"I blame myself . . ." cried Honeysuckle. "I should have seen what was going on from up here. I could have warned everyone with my honey-trumpet!"

"There, there," said Jasmine, patting his shoulder.

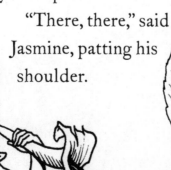

"I have a bird's-eye view from the top of my wooden trellis and I didn't see a thing either. Whoever's done this must be very, very clever indeed."

When the elves overheard these conversations, they smiled. It was about time the fairies realized how intelligent they were. Filled with pride, they continued with their mischievous plan, moving flowers here, there, and everywhere to make room for Tansy.

\* \* \*

But although the three elves were clever, they were also very tired. And because they were so tired, they began to make silly mistakes ...

One starry night, they dug up a patch of buttercups and instead of planting them on open ground, where they could enjoy the sun; they popped them under the trailing branches of the willow tree. It seemed wrong to leave the sleeping Buttercup behind, so they moved her too, giggling as she murmured in her sleep.

"What's going on?" shrieked Buttercup the next morning. She had woken to find that rather than being surrounded by the bright yellow faces of her flowers, she was in the middle of a group of tightly shut buds. "Why is it so cold?' she demanded of anyone who would listen. "Where is the sun? And, more importantly, why am I under a *tree*?" She was very confused and very, very cross.

In their eagerness to create space for Tansy, the elves had forgotten one of the most important things about the Flower Fairies' Garden . . . Some flowers liked the sun and some adored the shade, some liked to live in stone walls and some preferred rough ground, but every single flower had somewhere they truly belonged. Now the elves had messed up the garden, everything was in the wrong place.

The turning point came when the elves moved the beautiful yellow irises from their waterside home to the top of a windy ridge. Iris had joined Poppy for a sleepover in her delightful meadow. And when Iris returned to the garden the next morning, she stared and stared at the empty bank beside the stream. *Where had her flowers gone?*

A search party was organized and, moments later, Iris's beloved flowers were

found and replanted near the stream. But it took some time for the timid Flower Fairy to cheer up. "I th-th-thought I'd lost them f-f-forever!" she sobbed into her flower. "I th-th-thought I was h-h-homeless!"

Something had to be done.

So, one morning, not long after the elves had departed for their home next

to the lane, on the edge of the marshes, the
Flower Fairies held an emergency meeting
beneath the blackthorn bush. It was such an
important meeting that Queen of the Meadow
herself came to take charge. She and Kingcup
ruled Flower Fairyland together, making
sure that all of their fairy subjects were happy.
Now, they most certainly were *not*.

"Please tell me what has been going on."
The queen of the fairies spoke in a soothing

voice that made everyone feel better right away.

Candytuft was the first to speak. "We've been visited by mysterious intruders!" she said. "They pruned my flower without my permission. And I want to know who *they* are."

The Queen of the Meadow nodded, her necklace of green pearls clinking together as she tilted her head.

Shyly, Iris stuck her hand in the air.

"Th-they moved my flowers while I wasn't there," she said.

"They moved my flowers when I *was* there!" spluttered Buttercup. "And they moved me too!"

There were gasps of astonishment at each revelation. This wasn't the sort of thing that usually went on in the Flower Fairies' Garden. It was decided that all usual activities would be suspended for the day. There would be no gardening— the mysterious intruders had done quite enough of that. Neither would there be any parties, flying practice, or fairy-dust production. All efforts would be concentrated on discovering who had been making mischief in the Flower Fairies Garden.

"I shall set a trip wire made of spiderweb," announced Rose, who suspected the moles.

Almond Blossom, who thought the naughty crows had done it, decided to make a telescope. She used a hollow reed and placed a drop of dew at one end to act as a lens. Then she settled herself among Honeysuckle's

branches to wait for the intruders. Lavender, Zinnia, Jasmine, Sweet Pea, Poppy, and the rest of the Flower Fairies stood guard all around the edges of the garden.

They were ready.

## Chapter Five
## Discovered

The elves were so very tired nowadays.
During the day, they had trouble staying
awake. And if they'd eaten a big lunch, they
were sleepier than ever. They were dozing
among the toadstools while the Flower
Fairies' meeting took place, so they had
no idea that the little creatures were on the
lookout for them. At nightfall, they returned

to the garden once more, this time ready
to relocate the sunflowers to a shady spot
beneath the nightshade bush. There was
so much more room for them there.

It was almost too easy for the Flower
Fairies. No sooner had the first elf dug his
spade into the soil than Rose's small, lilting
voice cried, "Aha!"

At this signal, the elves were dazzled by
a hundred shining lights. It was the trusty
glow-worms. They had been waiting with
the fairies, ready to illuminate the crime
scene with their fiery tails.

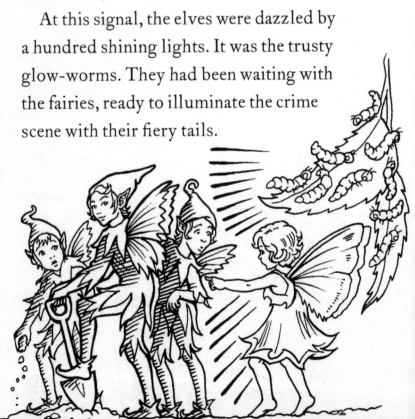

"Hi there!" said the chief elf, as calmly as if he were discovered digging up plants in the Flower Fairies' Garden every night of the week. "Took your time, didn't you? I thought you'd never work it out."

His fellow elves stared at him.

"You what?" spluttered the surprised medium-sized elf.

"You wanted us to be caught?" The smallest elf opened his eyes wide with astonishment.

The elf-in-charge set down his spade and wiped his brow. He addressed the watching Flower Fairies. "Look, why don't we all relax with a nutshell of elderberry juice?" The elf paused to give his audience a winning smile before continuing. "And then I'll explain."

Kingcup couldn't help chuckling at the cheeky elf's request. "I suggest you explain *first*," he said sternly, the edge of his mouth twitching.

\* \* \*

A short time later, just as dawn was breaking, the elves were sitting cross-legged at the center of the huge area they'd cleared. Before them were Kingcup and Queen of the Meadow.

And all around were
curious Flower Fairies—
some sitting, some perching on
low branches to get a better view, and
some hopping impatiently from one foot
to the other. Everyone was very interested to
hear what the mischief-makers had to say.

"I'm confused," said Kingcup, rubbing
his chin. "I really didn't think the elves were
fond of gardening. Could you start at the
very beginning and tell me what's been
going on?"

The watching
fairies turned
to each other,
expressions of
surprise and
bewilderment
on their faces.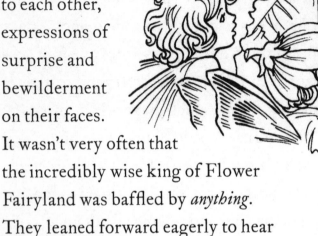
It wasn't very often that
the incredibly wise king of Flower
Fairyland was baffled by *anything*.
They leaned forward eagerly to hear
the elves' story.

"It's simple," said the chief elf. "Dandelion
asked Tansy to leave the garden because
there wasn't room for her flowers. All we've
done is shifted things around a bit to make
better use of the space. And I think you'll
all agree—" here, he looked at the gathered
fairies for support—"that with a little careful
landscaping, there's more than enough

room for our very good friend to grow any number of flowers." He threw his arms wide to take in the area they'd cleared. It was now big enough to host the Midsummer Party *and* the Spring Party at the same time. "We wanted to be discovered—"

"Did we?" said the small elf, who looked just as puzzled as Kingcup.

"Of course," said the chief elf. "How else would we get the chance to show everyone that there was enough room for Tansy's flowers? It would have taken the Flower

Fairies weeks to work it out." And he winked.

"Ahhh . . ." said Kingcup. "Now I see."
He gave Dandelion a stern glance, who
was suddenly looking rather embarrassed.

"I was just trying to help," he murmured.

The Queen of the Meadow smiled at the
elves. "A very clever plan," she said.
"It seems that you had the best intentions,
even if your methods were a little . . .
unusual."

"Right," said chief elf. "But if you think
we're going to say sorry—"

"—then you'll be waiting a long time,"
finished the medium-sized elf with
the moustache, triumphantly.

There were gasps of dismay from the watching Flower Fairies. Were the naughty elves going to get off scot-free? This couldn't be allowed!

"What about my buttercups?" cried Buttercup. "They can't live in the shade!"

"And my irises," whispered Iris.

"And my dandelion clocks!" bellowed Dandelion. "They didn't ask to move house."

"Neither did Tansy," said the chief elf. He smiled broadly. His words had hit their mark and he knew it. The Flower Fairies were silent. It was quite true, of course. Poor Tansy had been banished from the Flower Fairies' Garden, the only home she'd ever known. Overcome by guilt, Iris began to sob, great shiny tears rolling down her

pretty face. She was quickly joined by the
Sweet Pea Fairies and Almond Blossom
and Wild Cherry and—

"STOP!" commanded a voice.

The voice was familiar and all of the
fairies turned round to see who had spoken.
But the speaker was silhouetted against
the rising sun, and no one could make
out who it was.

"Reveal yourself!" said Kingcup.

And, with a rustling of skirts, a
beautifully dressed fairy stepped
forward. She wore a gown so
stunning that it dazzled the eyes,
with a matching mask held up
to her face. The beautiful
skirt billowed outwards like a
great, fluffy cloud. It seemed
to be made from thousands
upon thousands of small

yellow flowers. Yet more flowers had been sewn on to a circle of fine, green leaves to make a shining crown.

"Good afternoon," said the wonderful creature. "I am sorry to interrupt your meeting. But I think you'll be very interested to hear what I have to say."

The Flower Fairies, who had spent a lot of time being dumbfounded recently, were speechless once more.

Who could it be?

## Chapter Six
## Petals and Fairy Gowns

Kingcup found his voice at last. "Who *are* you?" he said.

"Don't you recognize me?" said the new arrival, lowering her mask. "Have you forgotten me already?"

"Tansy . . . ?" said the fairy king uncertainly. "It sounds like you, but you look so . . . so . . . glamorous!"

Tansy's cheeks turned pink, and she bent her head. "Why, thank you," she said. She didn't think she'd ever been so embarrassed in her whole life. "I haven't come to show off. I've come to support my friends, the lovely elves."

Now it was the elves' turn to blush.

"We're not lovely," muttered the chief elf. "We're the elves!"

Tansy winked at him and turned to the Flower Fairies, who were watching her with goggle-eyes. "I didn't know about their mischievous plan, and I'm sorry for any disruption they've caused. But I do think it was very kind of them to try and help me. Will you please forgive them? I happen to know that they have hearts of gold."

"No, we don't," protested the medium-sized elf. "We're cheeky monkeys."

The third elf nodded. "We're very, very naughty."

At this, the watching Flower Fairies—including Tansy—burst into peals of laughter. Kingcup and Queen of the Meadow rose to their feet.

"There's nothing to forgive," said the queen, smiling. "These kind elves have shown us that it was quite wrong of us to ask you to move house. We should have tried harder to find room for your flowers."

Kingcup nodded. "We'd be honored if you'd return to the garden," he said. He held out a hand towards Tansy. "Do please come back."

"*Please*," begged Candytuft. "I'll make lots and lots of tansy toffee and use up all of your spare flowers!"

Lavender stepped forward. "We've missed you so much," she said. "I'm sorry I haven't

visited recently. I've been so anxious about
the mysterious intruders, you see."

"It hasn't been the same without you,"
added Dandelion. "I'm really sorry I asked
you to move. Can you ever forgive me?"

"Of course," said Tansy, giving him
a hug. Now was the moment she'd dreaded.
It was her chance to break the news to her
old friends. She took a deep breath and said,
"I've been busy—" Her next words were
bumped out by the crowd.

"Hip-hip hooray!" cheered the happy
Flower Fairies. "Tansy's coming back!"
They formed a long line and the elves
tagged on the end. Together, they all
began to dance merrily around the garden,
whooping and shouting as they went.

"Excuse me!' called Tansy. This wasn't

going at all as she'd planned. When no one heard, she shouted louder. "Slow down!" Still they didn't hear, so she cried, "STOP!"

Dandelion, who was leading the line of dancing fairies and elves, came to an abrupt halt. One by one, each tiny creature cannoned into the one in front of them. *Bang, bang, wallop!*

"What's wrong?" asked Cornflower, rubbing his nose.

"I'm terribly sorry, but I won't be coming back," replied Tansy. There, she'd said it. "I like it on the King's Highway, you see."

There was a brief pause, when all that could be heard was the tweeting and chirping of the birds as they performed the dawn chorus. Then Herb Robert broke the silence.

"Not coming back?" said the little fairy,

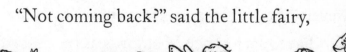

his brownish-pink wings fluttering nervously. He looked as if he might burst into tears.

"It's not that I didn't enjoy living in the Flower Fairies' Garden," she explained, smoothing her hands down her magnificent dress. "But I've discovered that living on the outside of it gives me so much free time."

"To do *what*?" asked Herb Robert, through trembling lips.

"I've always wanted to design and make wonderful clothes," explained Tansy, her eyes firmly fixed on the ground. When no one spoke, she continued. "I love mending clothes, but my dream has always been to make my own. Now I have so many spare flowers that I can make as many clothes as I like." Nervously, she raised her head and saw that every single fairy and elf was beaming at her.

The Queen of the Meadow was the first to speak. "How absolutely marvelous!" she exclaimed. "I think it's so important that everyone should follow their dreams and yours are so lovely. But are you absolutely sure that you don't want to come back?"

"Quite sure," Tansy said firmly. "I love you all dearly, but I love life on the King's Highway too. That's my home now." She smiled happily. "But remember that if any of you ever need a party dress or a magnificent suit of petals, you must visit me at once. I'd be delighted to create something splendid for each and every one of you."

And she did. Tansy could always be relied upon to make quite the most beautiful clothes any Flower Fairy had ever seen—and each and every one was decorated with a single tansy flower, just to show which happy little Flower Fairy had created it.

Visit our Flower Fairies website at:

# www.flowerfairies.com

There are lots of fun Flower Fairy games and activities for you to play, plus you can find out more about all your favorite fairy friends!

Log onto the
Flower Fairies
Friendship Ring

Visit the Flower Fairies website to sign up for the new Flower Fairies Friendship Ring!

★ No membership fee
★ News and updates
★ Every new friend receives a special gift!
(while supplies last)